What Are You Waiting For?

Scott Menchin

Pictures by Matt Phelan

A NEAL PORTER BOOK
ROARING BROOK PRESS
NEW YORK

For Yvetta and Karina —S. M.

For Nora and Jasper —M. P.

Text copyright © 2017 by Scott Menchin
Illustrations copyright © 2017 by Matt Phelan
A Neal Porter Book
Published by Roaring Brook Press
Roaring Brook Press is a division of Holtzbrinck Publishing Holdings Limited Partnership
175 Fifth Avenue, New York, New York 10010
The art for this book was created with pencil and pastel on toned paper.
mackids.com

Library of Congress Cataloging-in-Publication Data

Names: Menchin, Scott, author. | Phelan, Matt, illustrator.
Title: What are you waiting for? / Scott Menchin, Matt Phelan.
Description: First edition. | New York : Roaring Brook Press, 2017. |
   Summary: A badger finds his rabbit friend outside waiting for something
   and giving badger clues and guesses to figure out they are waiting to see
   the moon appear. | «A Neal Porter Book»
Identifiers: LCCN 2016035289 | ISBN 9781626721524 (hardback)
Subjects: | CYAC: Patience—Fiction. | Badgers—Fiction. | Rabbits—Fiction.
   | Friendship—Fiction. | BISAC: JUVENILE FICTION / Concepts / General. |
   JUVENILE FICTION / Bedtime & Dreams. | JUVENILE FICTION / Family / Parents.
Classification: LCC PZ7.M522 Wg 2017 | DDC [E]—dc23
LC record available at https://lccn.loc.gov/2016035289

Our books may be purchased in bulk for promotional, educational, or business use. Please
contact your local bookseller or the Macmillan Corporate and Premium Sales Department
at (800) 221-7945 ext. 5442 or by e-mail at MacmillanSpecialMarkets@macmillan.com

First edition 2017
Printed in China by RR Donnelley Asia Printing Solutions Ltd., Dongguan City, Guangdong Province

1 3 5 7 9 10 8 6 4 2

What are you doing up so early?

I'm waiting.

What are you waiting for?

Wouldn't you like to know.

Is it big?

What?

The thing you
are waiting for.

It can be.

So it's small?
    Sometimes.   Is it friendly?
                           When it smiles.

Does it have a mustache?

That's funny, but no!

Does it have eyes?

Yep! Sure does.

Does it have legs or a tail?

No legs! No tail!

Now I'm confused.
Can't you just tell me what it is?

That wouldn't be any fun.

Is it scary?
   I've seen it be scary.

                                    Is it quiet?
                                       Very quiet.

Does it have wings?

It can fly but doesn't have wings.

So it changes?

It's always changing.

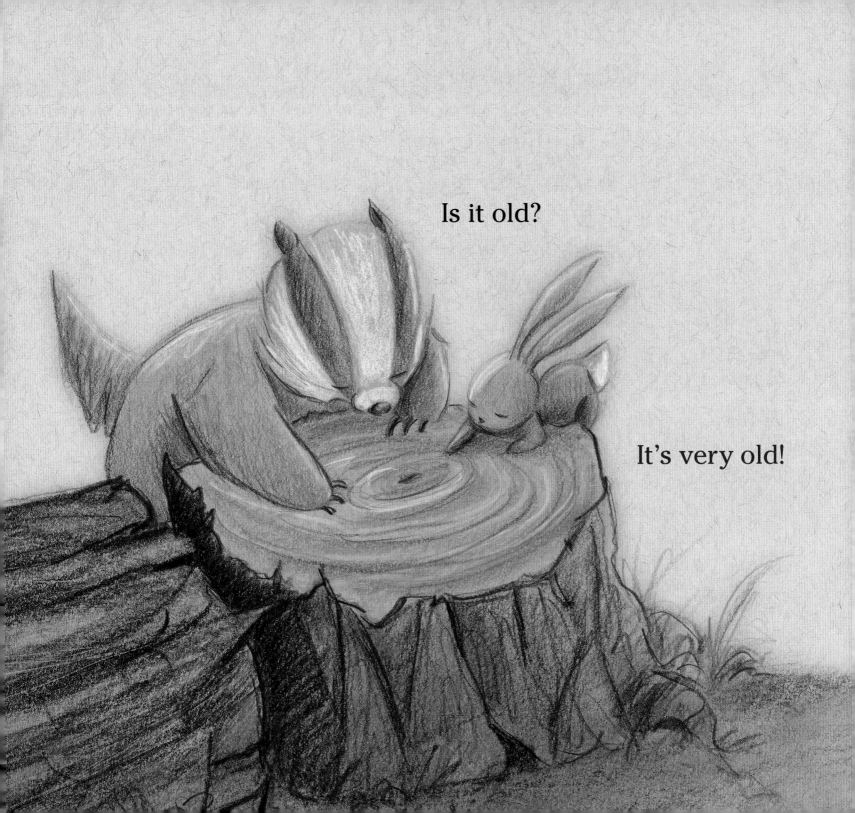

I'm so hungry.
Pretty please, tell me what it is.
Is it yummy?

No, it's not yummy.

Have you touched it?

Not me, but others have.

When will it come?

When it always comes.

I'm tired. I give up.

Don't give up now.
We waited all day.

Will I miss it if I blink?
What if I have to go to the bathroom?

       As long as you don't go to sleep,
       you won't miss it.

Okay. I'll jump up and down
on one foot so I don't fall asleep.

       I'll jump with you.

I guess jumping made him tired.

Oh no, I fell asleep.
Did I miss it? Did I miss it?

You woke up just in time.

I don't see anything.

Turn around.

WOW! It's everything you said it was.

I'm tired.

Let's go home.

Can we see it again tomorrow?
    Sure, but it might be different tomorrow.

Great! I love surprises.